The
Bat
in the
Manger

Written and Illustrated by
Diane Packard

AuthorHouse™
1663 Liberty Drive
Bloomington, IN 47403
www.authorhouse.com
Phone: 833-262-8899

Because of the dynamic nature of the Internet, any web addresses or links contained in
this book may have changed since publication and may no longer be valid. The views
expressed in this work are solely those of the author and do not necessarily reflect the
views of the publisher, and the publisher hereby disclaims any responsibility for them.

Any people depicted in stock imagery provided by Getty Images are models,
and such images are being used for illustrative purposes only.
Certain stock imagery © Getty Images.

This book is printed on acid-free paper.

ISBN: 978-1-6655-1699-0 (sc)
ISBN: 978-1-6655-1701-0 (hc)
ISBN: 978-1-6655-1700-3 (e)

Library of Congress Control Number: 2021903275

Print information available on the last page.

Published by AuthorHouse 02/26/2021

authorHOUSE

Foreword

In this story I wanted to show this historic moment in time from an aerial point of view. I chose the tomb bat for he was the only bat that eats insects in Egypt. During this time, a brilliant star was in the sky. By the end of my tale, a new light takes over the world. This book is dedicated to all that believe is Christ's miraculous birth.

In the spire of an ancient pyramid, lived Tut, a small furry tomb bat. Bright beams of starlight awoke him from his slumber. His chiropteran ears came alive upon hearing a distant sound. Tut's keen eyes plotted a flight course through the narrow window.

Surprised by a blast of wind and sand, Tut is whisked away with the storm. Whirling out of control not knowing up from down or east from west, the little bat felt helpless unable to use his echolocation.

Tut felt like just another grain of sand swept along the bank of the Nile river. Down by the river among the papyrus reeds, hordes of mosquitoes are also propelled into the sand storm. Seeing the mass of mosquitoes quickly reminds Tut of how hungry he really is.

Now on the ground below are the tents and humps of a traveling camel caravan. Hunkered down with eyes and nostrils sealed from breathing in the sand, the camels are unaware of our floating mammal above them.

The next thing Tut heard under him was the bleating of a flock of sheep being watched by shepherds.

Held hostage by the violent sandstorm, Tut
and the insects saw a dark crack into which they
could escape.

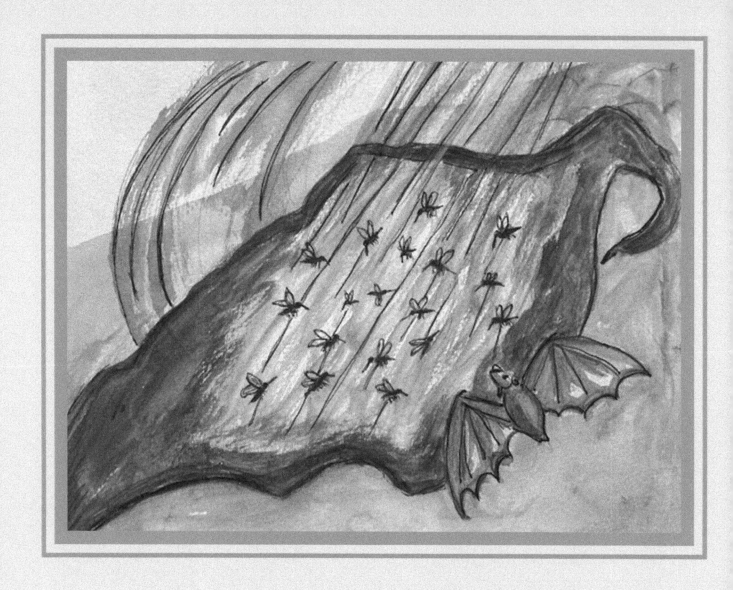

At the edge of the dark crevice, the swarming horde of mosquitoes were being sucked in like a huge magnet! Down, down, down, past the ceiling they were falling like they were shooting stars….

As a bat, tut knew just how to grasp the top edge of the grotto. Perched high above he had a perfect view of the scene happening beneath him.

All the animals gathered in the manger were getting very annoyed by all these biting mosquitoes. Tut realized that some of the mosquitoes could be carrying deadly diseases. Hearing his stomach growling, he unhooked his feet, unfurled his wings, and began hunting the pesky insects.

Tut grinned contentedly as he enjoyed inhaling mosquito after mosquito. Flipping the tasty morsels off the tip of his wings into his mouth, he can feel his hunger subside.

With his hunger under control he returns to
his roost high above the manger animals. All the
animals' heads turned toward the mouth of the
cavern as they heard two robed figures entering.

Just arriving outside the cave from an overcrowded town, Joseph and Mary are surprised to find such a cozy little den. What an inviting place to bring their new baby into the world.

It's so cool and dark inside the cave compared to the starlit desert night they just came from. The family-to-be settles on a sweet smelling, soft pile of hay.

From the top of the cave, two little beady eyes spies a lone mosquito making its way towards Mary. With one scoop, Tut snatches up the last of the nasty germ carrying mosquitoes, rescuing the family from deadly diseases.

Mary kneels as she tenderly places her newborn son on the sweet straw in the crib. Gradually the room seems to be coming alive with a new aura as the animals look on in awe.

Tut was so thankful to have helped the newborn King stay healthy from mosquitoes as he felt his gratitude go out like Light into all the world, joining the Love of the Christ-child.

Lightning Source UK Ltd.
Milton Keynes UK
UKHW020649090321
379992UK00002B/167